The Rock that Rolled Across the Ocean

Once there was a little rock covered with barnacles, seaweed and dirt. This little rock lived on a cold beach under a gray sky that rarely had any visitors at all.

Most days were quiet for the little rock as it laid lonely
on the dirty beach.

"I wish I could be something truly special," the rock would say
to itself, "but what could be special about a dirty rock covered
in barnacles?" So the rock simply sat and looked up at the sky.

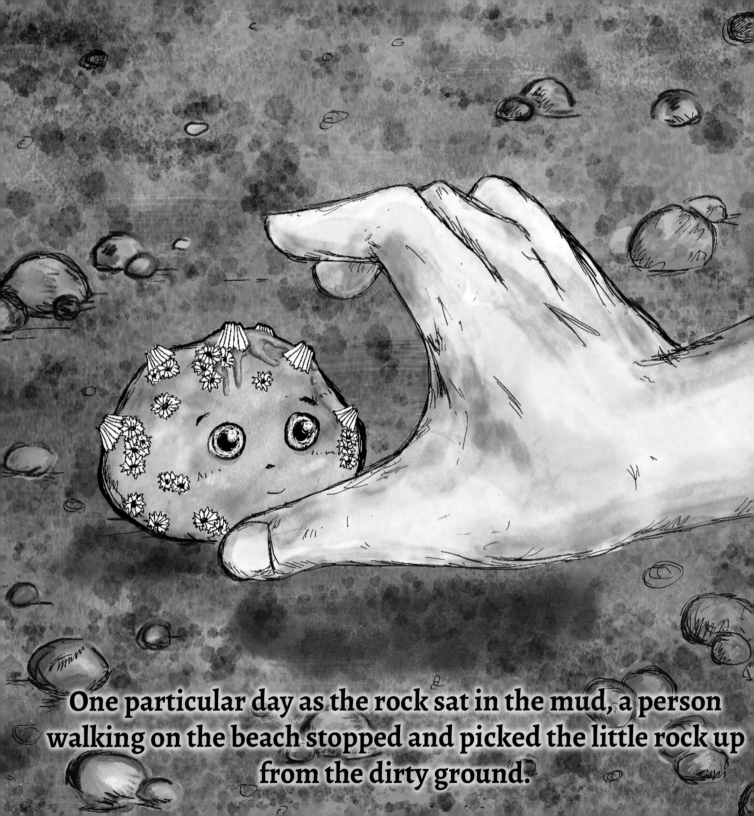

One particular day as the rock sat in the mud, a person walking on the beach stopped and picked the little rock up from the dirty ground.

"Hello little rock," the person said as they held it in their hand. "I'm so glad I found you! I have the perfect place for you!" Hearing this, the little rock felt as proud as a boulder! "You have a place for me?!" it asked as it stared up at the person. "Yes," the person said excitedly, "And, oh my, what a place it is!"

"Please understand though," said the person, "I can't take you with me now, but if you come find me across the ocean on the sandy shore, I will show you your purpose." And with that, the person set the little rock back down on the beach and walked away.

That night, the little rock couldn't sleep at all. "Should I start rolling across the ocean like the person told me? What if it's dangerous?" the little rock thought to itself. "No, I should go! I won't find my purpose standing still!"

So the little rock started rolling towards the ocean; rolling over dirty rocks, seaweed and garbage along the way, before finally reaching the water. "I've made it to the water," the little rock thought, "it shouldn't be long now!" And the rock kept rolling.

Some time passed and the rock continued to roll across the ocean floor. Further and further the rock rolled, and the water got deeper and deeper.

Later on, the little rock came to a big hill it could not go around, so it began to climb. "It shouldn't be long now!" thought the little rock as it neared the top of the hill. Suddenly, the rock heard a RUMBLE and saw a rockslide coming right at it!

With a **BASH** and a **SMASH** the rockslide hit the little rock, knocking its barnacles off and sending it tumbling backwards down the hill!

When the rockslide was over, the little rock sat sadly at the base of the hill once more. "I was so close to getting over the hill! Maybe I should quit and just go home," it thought to itself, but quickly changed its mind. "No! I have a purpose and that is where I need to be!"

So the little rock started up the hill again with a smile.

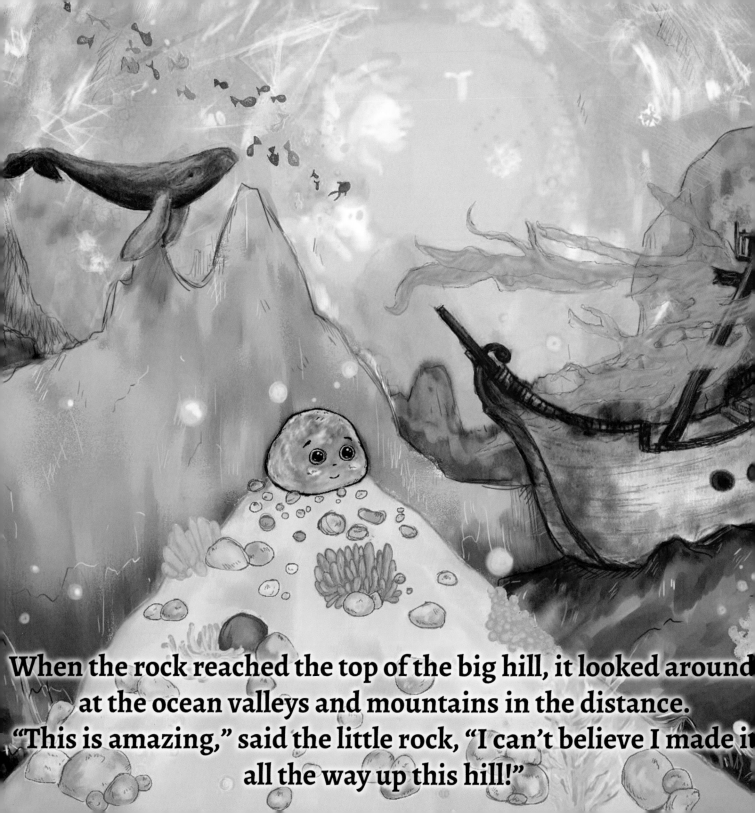

When the rock reached the top of the big hill, it looked around at the ocean valleys and mountains in the distance. "This is amazing," said the little rock, "I can't believe I made it all the way up this hill!"

hen, with a big smile, the little rock rolled down the other side of the hill, bouncing and laughing the entire way!

As the little rock journeyed onward, it noticed the water getting thicker and thicker with sand, but the rock kept rolling forward. "Shouldn't be long now," it thought to itself.

Before it could realize what was happening, the little rock
was caught up in a violent sandstorm;
pushing it from one direction to the next.

When the storm was over, the little rock sat on the ocean floor covered with sand and feeling very sorry for itself.

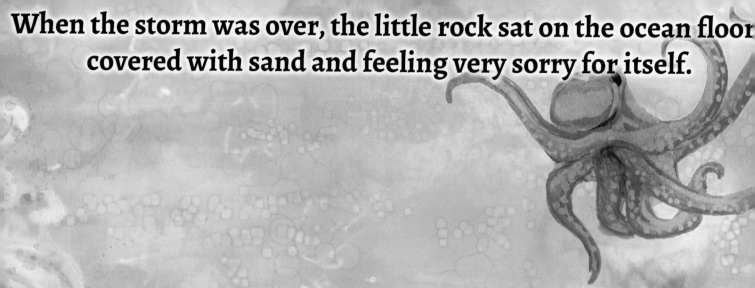

"Why do these things keep happening to me?" it said with a huff. "This was supposed to be easy but it is actually very hard! I can't stop though, the person is waiting for me and I need to keep rolling."

So the rock continued to roll forward; climbing hills and weathering sandstorms that weren't so much trouble anymore.

The little rock had traveled a very long distance by now and, as it admired a school of passing fish above it, the rock accidentally got stuck in a crack on the ocean floor.

"Oh no!" said the little rock as it tried to wiggle out of the hole "I'm stuck and I can't get out! Now I will never reach the sandy shore!"

Just then, the ground began to rumble and shake below the little rock. "What's going on?!" it asked, afraid of the rumbling below it.

Then, with a BOOM, a geyser blasted upward, launching the little rock out of the water and into the sky!

As the little rock sailed through the air, it saw something that
made it squeal with joy. "I see the sandy shore!" it yelled.
"It's right over there, not far at all!" and, with a plop,
the rock fell back in the water.

Returning to the ocean floor with a THUMP, the little rock could not contain its joy. "I can't believe I saw the sandy shore!" it said, and it started rolling once again.

When the rock finally reached the bright and sandy beach,
it smiled its biggest smile and looked around!
"I can't believe I made it!" it said happily.

As the rock sat in the sand looking up at the blue sky, the person saw it from far away and came running over!

Swooping the little rock out of the sand, the person held it tightly in their hand and smiled. "I'm so glad you found me, little rock!" the person exclaimed. "Now, let me show you your new home!"

Carefully and slowly, the person placed the rock down as the capstone above a beautiful sign. The little rock beamed with pride! It had finally found its purpose as a beautiful and polished rock.

Our journey prepares us
for our destination.
You are meant for great things;
don't stop rolling until you
find your purpose.

Thank you to Megan, Liam and my other wonderful family and friends who continually encourage me to keep rolling forward. I am eternally thankful God put you all in my life. - N.D. Byma

Previous titles include:
King Boogie
The Letter
Rahley the Silent Slug
Slightly Askew comic series

Website: www.ndbyma.com
Email: info@ndbyma.com